OVERTHINKER

THE NEVER ENDING FEELING

SONIA MARANDI

Made with ❤ on the Notion Press Platform
www.notionpress.com

Contents

Contents

Foreword

My goal is to entertain you all and show my creativity by writing books. Many people, like other types of stories but I like thrillers, suspicious, and crime stories. There are many stories I think I didn't know how to show to people so, I wrote stories that I like! and I hope you like my stories.

Preface

This story is going to be a lot for me because this story is inspired by my friend and me. No one really knows how I am feeling right now, and I can't just tell anyone about this. Until... I had an idea, to write about this so I can tell how I feel and spread awareness too... I am sure, everyone had felt this feeling once in their life (maybe) so it can be relateable for you all, I hope... The first half character development and scenes, all are inspired by the true events... while, the other half character development is based on my dearest friend, who really likes crime and murder, and she is a great inspiration for me. I really hope you enjoy this story...

-Author

Acknowledgements

Message from the author: I want to thank those who have helped in making my book! special thanks to the editor, she has helped me so much! she made all this for you. And again I want to thank them so much for helping me in making this book. Not to forget my viewers who read and view my books...

Prologue

In 2013, Mara Reia was ready to go to school, "Mara, take care and behave!" Mrs Reia said, "Mom! I am not a small kid, I know what to do, don't worry" Mara said and went to the school.

"Hey! Nia!" She tried to call her friend, but Nia ignored Mara... She felt awkward and went to her class. And everyone started laughing, "What's the matter? Why are you all laughing?" Mara asked, "Mara, in front of everyone trying to give a speech, nothing more embarrassing than that," They said, "How do you all know about that day!?" Mara asked, "Your bestfriend told us!" Mara wasn't happy to hear this, she was trying to go to her bench but she tripped and fell, "YOU ARE A LOSER!!" Mara started crying, "YEAH! CRY!" Mara wiped her tears and waited for Nia,

finally, Nia came. "NIA! Why did you tell them about that? That was 2 years ago!" Mara said, *"Just for fun!"* Nia said, "Fun? I didn't find it funny!" Mara said, "So, that's your problem!" "O-Of course it would be mine!" Mara said and her tears couldn't stop, "Mara! Stop this overacting!" Nia said and went away. No one came to help her, she stood up and sat in the corner, she saw everyone happy, "Will I ever be happy? I told lies to mom, All I just want is help! Happiness!" Mara thought and looked outside.

"Maybe it was all my fault, after all, I should have not given that speech, and I was the one to befriend Nia, so it's all my fault!" Mara again started crying. "Uh... Miss. Reia!" The teacher shouted, but it seemed Mara was busy thinking, "I did it..."

"Excuse me, Mara! I have been calling you, and you seemed to be in your imaginary world, now get out of my class!" The teacher said and everyone started laughing, "IT IS!! MY FAULT!! I am doing this to myself!" Mara couldn't stop crying.

Finally, the period was over and she could come to the class, while she was coming, she again tripped and fell, "Please!" Mara got scared, and everyone... started laughing like they always do. From that day, Mara had a fear of falling... She sat in her place, "I did that to myself, those problems they are having because of me! That's why I hate myself! I should die. What if I take a knife and stab myself? Head? Or Heart? What about the classic? Finding a rope wouldn't be difficult, and the fan, it's right here and the chair too" Mara smiled, "Why are you laughing?" Nia asked, "Why do you care?" Mara asked, Nia, didn't like it and slapped Mara in the face, "You can't ask questions!" Nia said, "Why? Are you doing Q&A with me?" Mara said, this made Nia very angry, she bet Mara... Mara was injured,

"All because of me..." She said, after school, she went to her home, refreshed, and went to the kitchen when her mother wasn't looking. She took the kitchen knife and analyzed it, after doing it, she got sad, "It's not sharp, it can't cut the skin... How am I supposed to do, I think I messed up, I need more ideas-" "What are you doing with that knife!?" Mrs Reia came, "Nothing..." Mara kept the knife and went to her room... "I think I am just thinking about things a lot, and I think it's called overthinking. Does that mean I am an *overthinker*?" Mara thought and couldn't stop thinking about it, sometimes she would feel curious, sometimes sad, sometimes angry... Oh dear, Mara Reia.

CHAPTER I

Mistakes can be done

In the year 2017, Mara was ready to go to high school. "I'm so excited!" She said, "Of course, dear," Mrs Reia said. She went to the high school only to notice Nia, her childhood friend. "Nia? What are you doing here?" Mara asked, "Mara, I know what I did to you in middle school, but that doesn't mean we can't be friends. I apologize, I am sorry" Nia said, "Oh?" Mara asked, "Yeah!" Nia said, "Okay... I accept your apology" Mara said and smiled. But, she didn't know *it was her biggest mistake...*

Mara went to the bathroom, inside the stall. Some girls came to the bathroom and started talking about Mara, she was hearing all that, "Do you know, Mara forgave Nia and they became friends again" Yasmine said, "Only to realize Nia was never her friend in the first place" Josie said and they started laughing, "What!? No way! Nia was never a real friend? Does that mean... she never cared about our friendship? No! No! This can't be true..." Mara thought, and she became sad. The girls went away and Mara went after them... Mara couldn't stop thinking about what she heard.

"Hey, Mara!" Nia said, "Oh... Nia" Mara replied. "Mara, can you do me a favour," Nia said, "Favour?" Mara asked, "Yeah... Can you do my homework?" Nia asked, "You know, you're good at mathematics, and I don't so..." "Oh... I can understand. Don't worry about that, I will do it" Mara said, "Thanks" Nia said and went away. "I guess it's okay to do favours. Friends can ask favours..." Mara thought.

After school, Mara went to find Nia, but Nia ignored her and left her there. Mara thought, who was still standing there, "Umm... well that's awkward" "Whom are you waiting for?" Yasmine and Josie came, "Nia. But she went away so, I will go alone" Mara said. "Oh! 'Will go alone. It's nothing new for you, right?" The girls started laughing, and Mara left.

"I am tired of being bullied! First at middle school and now... 'Oh Mara, you don't have friends blah blah. Friends don't mean anything to me, I would rather live alone!" Mara started overthinking, "But wait- if I don't want friends then, wouldn't t that make me a hypocrite*? I mean, still have a friend and- oh no, I again started overthinking. I should get home soon..." Mara thought and went home.

"So, dear, how was your high school?" Mrs Reia asked, "Uh, I don't know mom. What will you say if I told you, I forgave Nia and now we are friends" Mara asked, "I would say, you are an idiot!" Mrs Reia replied. "Sorry, mom. I didn't have any other choice. The only person I knew was Nia" Mara explained. "Mara, Nia is just like other girls, they just want to take advantage of you. They don't care about your friendship, they will ask hundreds of favours and will never even look at you! You would care about them, but they will not even give a damn about you! So, before she breaks your heart, it is better to forget her and ignore" Mrs Reia said, "Mom... these same things, I have heard it already" Mara said, "And you still became friends?" Mrs Reia asked, "Mom, I had doubts, what if she changed?" Mara said, "People like them never change!" Mrs Reia replied. "Dear, you still have time, tell Nia how you feel," Mara thought for a while, "Okay, mom," She said.

CHAPTER II

Incidents to overthink

The next day, Mara went to school, she was busy looking for Nia, "Hey! Who are you looking for?" Josie asked Mara, "Oh, I was looking for someone without a brain and here we are," Mara said, "Do you even know what are you saying?" Josie got angry, "Yeah, unlike you! Who spits crap from her mouth!" Mara didn't step backwards, she was ready to fight. "That's enough!" Josie also got ready for the fight, "I wish your parents would have said when they were raising you!" Mara replied. Josie punched Mara in the face, but, Mara defended herself. All started gathering to see the fight, Mara slapped and punched Josie so hard, she started crying. "Now who's the crybaby?!" Mara shouted. All were shocked, "Mara destroyed Josie!" All were saying.

"I can't waste more time here, I need to find Nia!" Mara thought and went to the class, she saw Nia, "Hey! Nia!" She shouted, "Oh, hi Mara!" Nia replied. Mara smiled and said, "You see... I don't like you ever since middle school, I have realized my mistake, I shouldn't have forgiven you yesterday. You want me so you can use me. It bothers me that you didn't care about me! Or our friendship, isn't it?" Mara said the truth. "Uhh..." Nia started stuttering, "Nia, I understand your real aim. You are no more my friend! Don't even try to talk with me!" Mara said and went away. Nia's other friends were seeing this, one forwarded her foot and made Mara trip, and she fell, "No! No!" Mara started screaming, and all started laughing, "Okay, Mara, it doesn't even bother me" Nia said and she went away. Mara stood up, wiped her tears, and sat on her bench, "Hey Mara! What did you say? Crybaby? Such a hypocrite! Who was crying after just tripping?" Josie laughed. Mara didn't feel nice and she became sad.

"What was I even thinking? Wow, I am so so cool. Look at me, I cried after tripping and getting bullied right after destroying Josie. Everyone laughed at me! I am an idiot! I am stupid! I just gave those bullies another reason to bully me. Because of this act, I just ruined my life more. IF ONLY I DIDN'T DO IT!! They were laughing at me... WHY? I DID THAT!? I should have just said her normally, at least it would have been less embarrassing after what I did. God! I just-" "Out of my class!" Mara walked outside of the class, "Great! Just like yesterday..." Mara started overthinking, and she became sad. And started feeling anxious, stressed, and worried.

Mara came inside the class, and again, all started laughing, "Mara, is it now your daily routine? Doesn't focus the class and then the teacher throws you out ?" They continued laughing. Mara became said. After school, she went home, "How was the day?" Mrs Reia asked, "Bad..." Mara replied, "Why?" Mrs Reia asked, "Everyone! They just bully me, how can it be good?" Mara said and started crying. "Dear..." Mrs Reia said in a soft voice, "Why don't we talk to the teacher?" "Oh yeah! And they will stop bullying me? Mom, when did life become so easy?" Mara explained. Mrs Reia became sad.

Maybe, the bullies were right, *it became a daily routine for Mara. Doesn't focus on the class and then the teacher throws her out.* This happened for many weeks, and the teacher also noticed this. 2 Months later, Mrs Ashford met Mara, "Mara? I have to meet your mother tomorrow" She said, "Okay Ma'am" Mara replied, "Mara, why aren't you focusing on the class?" Mrs Ashford asked, "I don't know ma'am, I just think about something and... just kept on thinking and thinking" Mara explained. "Hmm..." The next day, Mrs Reia came to Mrs Ashford's office.

"Mrs Reia, mother of Mara Reia?" Asked Mrs Ashford, "Yes, Mrs Ashford, you wanted to talk with me?" Mrs Reia asked. "Yes, it's about Mara. I hope she would have told you about this... but she isn't well focusing on class which makes her stand outside of the class, she said, she thinks about something and that's why she can't focus. Mrs Reia, I hope you talk with her and try to understand the problem. And, thank you for coming here" Mrs Ashford said, "I really didn't know about this, but I will try what I can do..." Mrs Reia said and went out, she got worried.

CHAPTER III

Mentally-ill: Mara Reia

Mrs Reia came to pick up Mara after school, Mrs. Reia wasn't looking happy like she always did, "Hey mom... did you come to pick me up? Never happened before" Mara said, "You have to give me some explanation," Mrs Reia said, they went home... on the way, "Mom? Why are you acting weird?" Mara asked, "I thought, you will tell me everything, and you didn't tell me what is happening to you," Mrs Reia said, "Mom, I already told you, I am getting bullied-" "Not that. About not focusing on the class" Mrs. Reia said, "Oh... that's what Mrs. Ashford told you. Ok mom, I admit, I didn't tell you about this. Not because I wanted to but because I have to. I didn't want you to worry about this, you are already worried about bullying, if I told you about this, you would get more worried, *I don't want that*, so... I just never told you about this, and... I am sorry" Mara said, "Next time, tell me all your problems, don't hide anything from me," Mrs. Reia said, "Ok mom," Mara said, they reached home and went inside.

"Go freshened up..." Mrs. Reia said and smiled, she took her phone and searched for something, "what do you call when you constantly think? Rumination? A habit of rumination can be *dangerous to your mental health*, as it can prolong or intensify *depression*" While reading this, Mrs. Reia wasn't feeling okay, she felt disturbed. "*Is it a disorder? Overthinking?*" She read more, she got more concerned. "No, if Mara is mentally-ill, I have to do something" Mrs. Reia, like any other mother, was too concerned about her daughter...

"Mara, be ready in five minutes," Mrs. Reia said, "Huh? Why mom?" Mara asked, "We are going to the doctor's," Mrs. Reia said, "What? Why? Are you okay, mom?" Mara got scared, "It's not about me, it's about you. Now go get ready" Mrs. Reia said, Mara, got ready but was still confused. Mrs. Reia started the car and they went to the Therapist. "Therapist?! What the hell mom?!" Mara shouted, "What do you think? Overthinking is not good!" Mrs. Reia said, "Overthinking? I was thinking, can't people now think?" Mara tried to explain, "What are you doing is not called thinking, *it's called overthinking!*' Mrs. Reia said, "You are just worrying too much about me, and mom, don't forget, I am 16 years old!" Mara said, "Whatever... now come with me, we will meet the doctor!" Mrs Reia said. They came inside Dr May's office.

"Natalie Reia?" Dr May asked, "Yes, doctor, I think my daughter is suffering from overthinking, I want to know what's the reason, she- she can't focus on her classes" Mrs Reia explained. "Oh... Mara, right? So, Mara, when did this 'overthinking' start?" "Two months ago...." "What do you usually think?" Mara looked at her mother and again at the doctor, "Before I think, some incidents happen with me, and they are those laughs, making fun, bullying me. I constantly think about them and blame myself. 'It's your fault!' 'You did this to yourself!' 'Because of you!' 'nobody loves you!' Kept on thinking, in the end, I accept it, I have made myself suffer, it's all my fault!" "Mara, I am gonna tell you some symptoms of depression, tell me you have it or not" "Okay" "Feelings of sadness, tearfulness, emptiness or hopelessness?-Yes, right now" "Angry outbursts, irritability or frustration, even over small matters-Yes, before meeting you, I shouted at my mom" "Loss of interest or pleasure in most or all normal activities, such as hobbies or sports?-

Yes, I haven't played football for a while" "Sleep disturbances?-Yes, I can't sleep till midnight" "Tiredness and lack of energy, so even small tasks take extra effort?-Yes, I don't want to do work" "Reduced weight?-Yes, I am underweight" "Feelings of worthlessness or guilt, fixating on past failures or self-blame?-Yes, just now told" "Trouble thinking, concentrating, making decisions and remembering things?-Yes, that's why I get punished" "Frequent or recurrent thoughts of death, suicidal thoughts, suicide attempts or suicide?-Yes, every day, I just want a sharp knife" "Unexplained physical problems, such as back pain or headaches?-Yes, no wonder I get random headaches" After few talks, the Doctor said, "Mrs Reia, with the symptoms your daughter said, and the talk, I can say, *your daughter is suffering with depression and that's why she is overthinking.* She has depression because of her personality, she blames herself, loneliness in school, and maybe bullying. And I am sorry to say, but, *depression can't be cured.* It can be treated by support, medications, therapy" The doctor said. Mara and Mrs Reia went away.

CHAPTER IV

I am my worst enemy

"So?" Mrs Reia asked, "It's not a big deal..." Mara said, "You think it's normal, but it isn't! What do you think depression is? A small thing?" Mrs Reia was fed up, "Yes, *what can be the worst thing to happen?*" Mara said, "Worst thing?! What did you say there? 'every day, I just want a sharp knife now, I understood why you had the knife that day. Dear, I am saying, you can't hurt yourself, if you hurt yourself, there's no point living with me too. I don't want to lose my daughter. *I just want to see you happy, smile*" Mrs Reia said, "Mom, I don't think you can see me like that..." Mara said and sat in the car, Mrs. Reia wasn't happy, she rode home. Mara went inside her room and started to draw something, Mrs. Reia came inside too and was shocked by it, "What the hell is this!?" She asked Mara didn't say anything, "These scribbles, this isn't looking nice" But, Mara didn't say anything, Mrs. Reia went away, "Now, she's acting weirder, I can't stop worrying about her" Mrs Reia said to herself.

The next day, Mara went to school, she reached the class and heard laughs, Mara wasn't feeling okay, she started screaming, "AAAH! STOP!! STOP LAUGHING!!!" All went silent for a moment, Mara began to cry, she covered her ears and fell. All were looking at her, everyone was confused. The class was going to start, and everyone went to their bench, Mara stopped crying, and she too went to her bench. "What the hell was that? Now everyone is going to think about that only? I am just an embarrassment for myself, everyone is gonna talk about me. I cried like a baby there, how can anyone be irritated by laughter? You can be! You idiot!" She started to think about all those negative things... The teacher saw Mara wasn't focusing, "She is still not focusing..." She thought.

It was lunch break, Mara was still lost in her mind. Suddenly, her classmates came, "Hey! Mara!" They shouted, Mara, looked at them, "What do you want from me?" Mara asked, "What the hell happened in the morning?" They asked, "Why do you care?" Mara asked, "You are weird!" They said Mara didn't say anything. "Anyways weirdo, we know you are mentally ill! You are doing all this for some attention! 'oh look, I have depression, help me" They said and started making fun of her, Mara was in shock, "How do you know about this?" She asked, "Your friend told us!" "Friend? Nia!" Mara went to find Nia, "What is your problem!?" Mara shouted, Nia, looked at Mara, "What happen?" She asked, "What happened you ask!? How do you know about my depression?" Mara asked, "I saw you at the doctor's, and what can go wrong with telling others? C'mon secrets aren't supposed to be by yourself, we should tell everyone" Nia said, Mara got angry, she saw a steel bottle on the table, took it, and smashed Nia's head, "How can you do that!" Mara said angrily, Nia fell, and all stared at her, "You deserve that!" Mara said and went away, "Hey! Look she is bleeding" Mara saw back, "Doing all these for some attention" and went to her bench, she started eating her lunch,

"Wait... what I just did, was it right? She told my truth to everyone without even asking me. If everyone knows, they would get another reason to bully me... I smashed her head, am I going to be in trouble? What if the principal knows? He would expel me from the school!" Mara got scared. Some children came to Mara, "Hey weird!" Mara looked at them, "What do you want from me?" Mara asked,

"Looks like someone is in trouble!" They said and started laughing. "What do you mean by that?" Mara asked, "Well... the principal has called you" "What? No NO NO!!" Mara got scared, "You don't believe us?" "NO! I DON'T!" "Why don't you ask others?" Mara ran to others, "Did the principal call?" Mara asked, "Yes, you should get going," The children said, Mara got nervous, and she ran to the principal's office only to find out... he was not there, "What the hell? Why is he not here?" Mara asked herself, she heard laughs and looked back... everyone was laughing at her. Mara got sad, she started crying, "Why did you all do this to me!" She asked, "*Just for fun!*" She got a flashback, 'NIA! Why did you tell them about that? That was 2 years ago!" Mara said, "*Just for fun!*' She wiped her wipes and went to the bathroom, inside the bathroom. She closed her mouth, so no one can hear her screams, and with the other hand, she continually wiped her tears. suddenly she heard footsteps, it was again, Yasmine and Josie... "My god! Mara is such a *drama queen*! 'oh look! I have depression!' All she wants is attention!" Yasmine said, "Yes! I agree!" Josie said. Meanwhile, Mara doubted herself, "I? I never wanted attention from anyone!" Mara got sad. After hours, Mara went out of the stall, "Oh... no" The school have ended. All were going out, she went to the classroom and took her bag and went home, she looked into her eyes, "Man, I look tired" Her eyes were red.

She reached home, "Hello Dear," Mrs Reia said, "How was the" "It was horrible! Nia knew about my depression, she told everyone and they... they bullied me! They said I am doing this for some attention! Now they wouldn't stop making fun of me!" Mara cried. "Maybe, it's all my fault!" "No. Dear, you did nothing wrong, why are you blaming yourself?" Mrs Reia asked, "Because I am the problem!" "What the hell are you talking about? You are not a problem, they are the problem!" Mrs Reia tried to make her understand, but, Mara wouldn't listen. "Okay, tell me what you did wrong?" Mrs Reia had enough, "Who overthinks all the time which led to depression? I! Who gave them another reason to them to bully me? I!" Mara said and went to her room. "Feelings of worthlessness or guilt, fixating on past failures or self-blame..." Mrs Reia thought.

CHAPTER V

I am happy, is it a problem?

It was Sunday, Mara, and Mrs. Reia went to the nearby park. "Is it refreshing out here?" Mrs. Reia said, but, Mara didn't respond, instead, she was overthinking, "Mara?" "Yes, mom" "Dear, you need to stop thinking about the past. We can't change them, and there's no point in thinking about them, so why don't we think about our future" Mrs. Reia said. "That's the problem mom, I can't" Mrs. Reia became sad. They went for a walk, enjoying it, until, Mara got distracted by a *dead rat,* "Mom, look a dead rat!" Mara said, "Don't touch it!" Mrs. Reia said. *Mara smiled,* "Wait? Did you smile?" Mrs. Reia asked, "Did I? *I like corpses*" Mara said, Mrs. Reia got scared, "Corpses? That is not good..." She said. "Whatever you say, mom..." Mara said. And they continued their walk...

The next day, Mara went to school, it was her biology class. "Okay, students, we are going to do practicals today!" The teacher said, "Practical? Eww... Who loves to kill animals?" Everyone said, Mara heard it, "Eww? What's disgusting about that?" She thought. "Okay, who is ready for the practical on this rat?" No one was interested, except Mara. She took the small needle, and cut right through it, "No NO! You should not do that! You killed that rat!" The teacher said, "Oh... I am sorry, teacher. I will do it again" Mara said, she did it again, and it was correct. "Good, Mara" The teacher smiled. Mara became happy.

The biology class ended, and no one was happy about it. Yasmine and Josie were gossiping in the bathroom, "To be honest, the class was boring!" Yasmine said, "Yes!" Josie agreed, "Yasmine, did you see Mara? How is that possible? She was happy today" "Happy today?" Nia came, "Yes, Nia. She was the only student who seemed interested in that class" Yasmine said, "She was sad and depressed for so many months, and now she is happy? WOW!" Nia said. Chameleon changing her colors!" Nia said, Yasmine and Josie agreed.

They went to class, "Hey weird Chameleon!" Mara didn't listen to them. "I am talking to you!" "What do you want?" Mara was annoyed. "You were sad a few days ago, how are you happy today?" Nia said, "What now? I can't be happy now?" Mara said, "Yes!" Nia said, "WOW!! You aren't happy because I am happy, jealous b- whoops, can't you stop being an obstacle for me? I mean, I want to be happy, and because of people like you, depressed people can't be happy or cured! What? You wanted to bully people! But, don't forget what I did to that rat, I didn't hesitate in taking the sharpest knife or needle and killing with you" This made Nia get scared and run away, "Yeah run away you little-" Mara said and laughed... "Man, this is such a good day! I wish my other days will be like this" She thought.

The school ended, and Mara went home, feeling very happy, "Mom! Guess what? Your daughter is happy today?" Mara said, "Oh, good to hear, so, tell me what happened that made you happy?" Mrs. Reia asked, "So... there was a biology practical where we have to cut a rat and do some surgery. But I liked when I killed that rat!" Mara said and smiled. "Oh... if you are happy with that, I am happy for you" Mrs. Reia smiled but was scared. "And then, annoying Nia came to me, said 'I don't want you to be happy' so I threatened and scared her by saying 'I can kill you without hesitation' and then, she ran like a-" "Oh great! She deserved that!" Both were happy. "Mom, I just wish, I see myself happy every day!" Mara said, "Me too, see my daughter happy," Mrs. Reia said, "Then, I will become a great surgeon!" Mara said.

15

CHAPTER VI

Happiness is not permenant

The next day, Mara went to school and was very happy. But, everyone knows, *Mara can never always be happy...* Nia came to her, with an angry face, "What do you think? You can threaten me, and then just run away?" She said, "No one can mess with Nia Micheals!" "What the hell are you talking about?" Mara was confused. "Miss. Mara Reia, please come to the office," The announcer said. "Now go!" Nia said, Mara went to the office and saw the principal...

"Sir, you called me?" Mara asked, "Yes. You violated our rules" The principal said, "What rule?" Mara asked, "No violence in this school" "But, sir, I never did any violence" Mara got nervous, "Oh, really? May I make you remember? You smashed Nia Micheals's head with a 'steel bottle' Do you know how dangerous it is?!" "But sir-" "Here's your letter" The principal handed a letter to Mara, "Suspended for a week!?" Mara was surprised, "Now, no more time wasting, you can go" Mara went outside, very sad... Meanwhile, Nia and her friends were busy laughing at her.

On the way to home, Mara started crying, "I knew this would happen! I shouldn't have done that to Nia. But it was days ago... how did the principal know? Oh, Nia would have complained to him. Such a... ALL BECAUSE OF ME!! WHY DID I DO THAT!!!" She asked herself... Finally, she reached home. She rang the doorbell, Mrs. Reia came to open it and had a surprised face

"What are you doing here? You were supposed to be in the school" Mrs. Reia said, "Well, I am suspended" Mara replied, "What? Why?" Mrs. Reia asked, "Apparently that

Nia complained to the principal and he called me and..." "For how many days are you going to be at home?" Mrs. Reia asked, "A week" Mara replied. "You want anything?" "No... I am not in the mood" "Take rest in your room" Mrs. Reia got worried, "This is going to make her worse, she is now feeling more guilty, and she is going to blame herself more, which means, she is going to be sadder" Mrs. Reia thought...

It was afternoon, "Dear, it's lunchtime!" Mrs. Reia called Mara, she washed her hands and sat in the dining table's chair, ready for her meal, suddenly, she got scared, and started shivering. Mrs. Reia noticed it, "What happened, Dear?" Mrs. Reia asked, Mara was still shivering, scared and tears started dropping, "Dear!?" Mrs. Reia got more scared. "AAAH!! STOP LAUGHING!!!" Mara covered her ears and fell, Mrs. Reia picked her up... and took a glass of water, "Here, drink" Mrs. Reia gave the glass of water to Mara, and she drank. "Be calm, what happened to you now?" Mrs. Reia asked, Mara couldn't stop crying, she hugged her mother, "They are laughing at me!" She said, "Who is laughing at you?" Mrs. Reia asked, "My classmates! I did this to myself, right? I did this to myself" Mara started to blame herself, "No, no! You did nothing" Mrs. Reia said. A few minutes later, Mara stopped crying, but was still, scared. "How are you feeling now?" Mrs. Reia asked, Mara, didn't respond. "Okay. Dear, there's no one here, we are at home, why did you think that people are laughing at you?" Mrs. Reia asked, "Because of that thing" Mara pointed to a *steel bottle,* and Mrs. Reia understood, "She remembered because she smashed Nia with a steel bottle, and then, they laughed at her. No... it became a trauma for her, when she thinks related to it, she remembers that time, no!" Mrs. Reia got worried. Mrs. Reia thought this will end soon, but... Mara got these types of flashbacks for a month and a half, Mrs. Reia decided to go to the therapist's

They came inside, "Mrs. Natalie Reia, how's the depression?" Dr. May asked, "I think my Mara is getting worse," Mrs. Reia said, "Why do you think so?" Dr. May asked, "It's been a month, and my daughter is seeing nightmares of an awful event, if she does anything related to it, she gets scared. She would get flashbacks of that day, and her overthinking wouldn't stop. She changed a little, and always blame herself" Mrs. Reia said. "Bring Mara, I need to talk" Mrs. Reia brought Mara, "Young girl... how do you feel when you remember those flashbacks?" "I will feel scared and start shivering and crying. Then, I think negative thoughts about myself, if I hear laughs or see a steel bottle, I start crying. I don't feel like living" Mara said, "I think your mother was correct, it was a traumatic experience for you, I believe you also have PTSD, and it's treatable, after coming from school, talk with your mother about what happens, if you have any flashback, talk about that to your mother, and you can take some medications like Antidepressants, Anti-anxiety medications, Prazosin" The doctor said, "Thank you, doc" Mrs. Reia said and they went away...

CHAPTER VII

Different from others

Look like finally, Mara's luck changed. For many months, she didn't have any flashbacks or mental breakdowns. And, focused on the class, "Mara, you started focusing more, good!" Mrs. Ashford would say, Mara was happy, she would ignore Nia and others, tell good things that happened to her mother, and after 2 years later, in the year 2019, she completed high school, one of the best days for her. It was time to apply for a college, "How about V.K. Medical college?" Mara asked her mother, "Okay... Do they teach well?" Mrs. Reia asked, "Of course mom!" Mara replied. Mara tried to apply to the college, "So I just have to write a good essay and do some work, I hope they select me" Mara hoped, "Of course, they will select, you brought the best marks in the exam, how can they not select you?" Mrs. Reia boosted her confidence. A few months later, she got a letter, "Dear, you got a letter from... V.K. Medical college?!" "Wait??" Mara got excited, "Dear, Mara Reia..." Mara started reading the letter, "Congratulations, you are selected!!!" Mara got happy and couldn't stop herself to dance, "Yay!!" "Congrats dear!" Another best day for her...

The next day, Mara got ready for her first day of college, she reached the college... and went to her class. "Okay, a surgery class," Mara thought and took her note and started taking notes, she focused well in the class. After the class, she met someone, "Hey, are you a new student?" A guy from her class asked, "Yeah, today is my first day" Mara replied, "My name is Eric Nelson, nice to meet you" Eric said, "My name is Mara Reia" Mara replied, "Wow, such a cool name!" Eric said, Mara was surprised, "No one ever said me that," Mara said, "What? Why?" "Yeah, they made fun of me" "Oh just ignore them... by the way, are you learning surgery?" Eric asked, "Yes, are you too?" Mara asked, "Yes!" Both seemed happy, "The next class is after one hour, and it's lunchtime. Why don't we grab some food and eat together?" Eric asked, "Sure, I would love to..." Mara replied. They both talked for a while and became friends...

"Hey, mom! Mom, you wouldn't believe it, I met a guy, his name is Eric Nelson. He is very kind! And study surgery!" Mara said to Mrs. Reia, "That's great, but I fear he would be like Nia..." Mrs. Reia said, "Me too, I hope he wouldn't be like that..." Mara said and ended the call, "Sorry, but I may overhear your conversation, I don't want to be much personal, but who's Nia?" Eric said, "Why don't we tell each other about ourselves, I will tell you," Mara said, "Okay, I will go first. So, I was born in a village, a low caste, different religion, and... I was discriminated against by my caste and everything for my whole life, I was left alone, no one became my friend, and teachers hated me. I lived alone... although I am good at studies, they never appreciated me..." Eric said with a sad tone. "I am sorry to hear that, my story was too same as yours, I was betrayed by my own best friend, Nia. The whole class hated me for no reason and bullied me, because of that I had depression and PTSD for many- like 5 years. I somehow got treated" Mara said, "You suffered more than me..." Eric said. "The next class is going to start, let's go" Mara and Eric went. "Mara, thanks!" Eric said, "What? Why are you saying thanks to me?" Mara was confused, "You are my first friend, and accepted me as who I am," Eric said, "After 18 years?!" Mara asked, "Yes.." He agreed, both smiled, and went to the class.

CHAPTER VIII

Another one

After the class, they met a girl, "Hi you both" The girl said, Eric and Mara, looked at each other, "Hi...?" They said, "I am Helen Robins," Helen said, "Hi..." They said awkwardly, "Actually I am new here, and need some friends, so can you both be friends of mine?" Helen asked, "I am sure, I didn't see you in this lecture," Eric said, "Because I am an anesthesiology student," Helen said, "Then you should make friends with other anesthesiology students, and we are surgery students," Mara said, "I would, but they are not willing, please! I just want some friends!" Helen said, "Okay, I mean *what can be the worst thing to happen?*" Eric said. "Thank you! What's your name?" Helen asked, "I'm Mara and he's Eric," Mara said...

A few hours later, when College ended, they went for a walk, "So... you guys ever felt betrayal? From your partner or friend?" Helen asked, "Oh, I had! From a friend, she made fun of me because others would do" Mara said, "Oh so sad. My friends left me because I offended them sometimes" Helen said, "Offended? What do you mean by that?" Eric asked, "I would joke about something and they would get easily offended" Helen explained, "Oh..." Mara and Eric said.

While they were busy talking and walking, Mara saw a group of students staring at them, "Guys, those people on the left seem staring at us" Mara said, "Yeah, I also think..." Eric said. "What? They would probably be looking at something else..." Helen said nervously, "No, see, they are looking at us only!" Mara said, "Let me just talk to them..." Eric said, "No need!" Helen tried to stop him, "Why?" Mara asked, "I-it's not necessary," Helen said, "Helen, why are you slurring?" Mara got suspicious.

Eric went towards the group, "Hey fellas! Is there any problem? It seem you were staring at us..." Eric said, "Oh brother, there's no problem with you, it's about that girl, Helen Robins..." The group said, "She just wants us to be jealous..." A girl from the group said. "What? Sorry, but I can't understand" Eric said, "Look, that girl! She's using you and your other friends. She wants her old friends to be jealous, like 'omg you have new friends, I am jealous' it's like a relationship. The reason we left her was she made very offensive jokes, she didn't know the limits and moreover, she wouldn't even care about your friendship!" The group said, Eric was shocked to hear, "What?" Eric couldn't believe it, he looked back, Mara and Helen were talking... "Brother, if you don't believe us, just stay with her for some days or weeks, and she would be another person, whom you will hate the most!" The group said. "Okay... thanks," Eric said, and went towards Mara, "Hey Mara, can we talk for a moment?" Eric asked, "Okay?" Mara said and went a little away, "So?" Mara asked, "That group was her old friends, they told me Helen isn't a good friend, in fact, she is the worst," Eric told everything that the group told him. "I don't know what to say... Let's wait up for a while" Mara said... Eric and Mara went to Helen, "Our class is going to start, we will see you later..." They said and went away. They were a little upset. Later, "Hi, Mom," Mara said, "I met a girl, her name is Helen Robins, I thought she is innocent, but her old friends told her secret, I am confused, so... I will just wait some days and see myself," Mara said, she was talking to Mrs. Reia...

The next day, Helen came to them, "Hey! How's your class?" Helen asked, "Mine was very awful, I mean a girl, she thought of herself as a model, I mean who wears makeup, she just wants to attract other guys! I also have a big crush on this guy, he looks very cute" Helen kept talking, but Eric and Mara couldn't talk... Later, they talked about their past, "I didn't struggle much, because I was the popular girl in the high school and everyone loved me, so I can't relate to you both" Helen said. Helen would sometimes make jokes about Eric or Mara since they are friends, it's not a big deal, right? This happened for weeks, maybe her old friends were right. Mara didn't like it, she felt she is no one. One day so happened...

"Hey Eric, how would your school discriminate against you? Not allow you to enter?" Helen said and laughed, "Helen, you know it's very offensive! And, it's not even funny!" Mara said, "Why are you telling me what to do? You know, there's no difference between you and mental, because you are 'mental'lly-ill" Helen said and continued to laugh, Mara had enough, "That's enough! Your old friends were right! It's time to spit some facts! You are annoying as hell! I mean, you would talk more about others than yourself, the last time you talked about yourself, is how popular you are! You don't know any struggle, if you don't know at least you should how to act to a struggling person! You made thousands of 'offensive' jokes about me and Eric, how would you understand how it feels? You used us! You make us walk in front of your old friends so you can make them jealous, gossip and all, you don't even study, why are you in this college? I don't want to be your friend anymore, you can get the- you can go and never talk with us, you bring your new friends, walk in front of us, we don't care! Now, get out!" Mara said angrily, "I have a question, were you always this angry?" Helen said and took her steel bottle and drank from it, Mara paused, she remembered the bad memories, and she started shivering and got scared, "AAAAH!!! STOP LAUGHING!!" She covered her ears and fell, "Mara!" Eric said and hugged Mara, "Be calm... forget it. Remember the last time you were happy" Eric said, Mara started thinking, "My name is Mara Reia" Mara replied, "Wow, such a cool name!" Eric said, Mara was surprised, "No one ever said to me that," Mara said... Mara passed out, "Mara?" Eric sprinkled water on Mara, and Mara woke up, "Thanks" She said, "Don't worry, how are you feeling now? Here, take some water" Eric gave the glass bottle to Mara, She drank it, "I'm feeling okay..." Mara said, she stood up, "Mara, you can talk with your mother, shall I buy some juice for you?" Eric said, "No need" Mara replied, Eric went away to buy some juice for himself...

"I guess he's right. I should talk to mom, that feeling was horrible" Mara said. Mara took her phone, and called Mrs. Reia, "Hey? Mom?" "How are you? Dear" "Good, something messed up happened today. So, weeks ago, I told you about Helen, well that Chameleon showed her true face, and now I hate her, she knew I am a PTSD patient, still, she made me remember those memories, I was scared and even screamed!" "Then?!" "Eric told me to think about a good memory, I remembered how he complimented me when we first met, then I passed out and woke up, and he told me to call you and talk about this..." "Wow, he's such a caring guy" "Mara!" Eric shouted, "Looks like he came, I will talk to you at home, love you mom" Mara ended the call, "Two juice?" Mara asked, "I know you didn't want it, but I bought it anyways," Eric said and gave a juice to Mara, "Thanks!" Mara replied, and they sat on a bench and drank the juice...

CHAPTER IX

The Past is not leaving me

Although everything was happy for Mara, she met many bullies in college too, why did they bully her? Because she was too good, and they were jealous, they would also like to annoy her. She tries to ignore them, but couldn't... "Kenneth! Can you just let me do my thing?" She would get fed up. Who were they? Shawn Verne, Andy Maltin, and Kenneth Foster. "Hey, do you need some help?" Andy asked, "Oh, it would be great!" Mara said but, Andy threw the things, and they laughed, and Mara became sad and picked up the thing. "Hey! Mara, what do you think who are you?" Shawn said, "But I did nothing!" Mara always felt sad...

One day, Mara couldn't find a lab, she saw a guy and asked him, "Hey do you know where the laboratory is?" "Of course!" The guy said, he touched her hand inappropriately, and she started feeling uncomfortable, "Excuse me, don't touch my hand!" Mara said and ran away from that person... "Hey, are you okay?" A girl asked her, "That guy, his name is Norman Spencer. He will always harass girls in any way, good you ran away" The girl said, "Oh..." Mara said, "What's your name?" The girl asked, "I am Ida Jameson" Ida said, Mara thought she can be a good friend, as she too was a surgery student but... "Can you give me the notes for today?" "What? Weren't you in the class?" "I bunked" Ida used Mara... She would ask for notes every day until, one day Mara broke her friendship with her, "If you want to use someone, go find others, **sorry but your worker is quitting!**" Mara said...

In the year 2022, it was Mara's 4ᵗʰ year, she was in the hospital, busy doing her work until she saw the hateful, Nia Micheals, "What the-" Mara said, she tried to avoid her but she came to her, "Oh, so you are working here?" Nia said, "What's your problem? Why are you here?" Mara asked angrily, "To meet my friend, Ida!" Nia said, "Oh that Worker haver?" Mara said, "You are still like this?" Nia asked, "You too, don't forget if you did anything funny I don't hesitate in taking the sharpest knife or needle and kill you!" Mara threatened, "Still threatening me? I bet you can't even do that!" Nia laughed, Mara was pissed off, "Let's see..." Mara said... The next day, Mara wasn't feeling nice, "Hey, you seem unhappy. Is it the studies? Or hospital?" Eric asked, "I met my worst enemy!" "Nia? Don't overthink about her! Why don't we study the 13ᵗʰ Chapter? Or we can go for a walk?" Eric suggested, "Walk will be good" Mara smiled and they went for a walk and talked for a while, she forgot about Nia. That's what she thought...

The next day, She again met Nia, "Hey! Weirdo! Are you still that depressed weirdo?" Nia said, "Just ignore her..." Eric said and they went away, "Hey..." Here comes Norman, "Leave me alone!" Mara said, she felt weird, "Eric? Eric?" Mara couldn't see Eric, the whole place was dark, All that she could hear was "HAHA!!" Mara stopped, "Are they laughing at me? Who is laughing at me? She is right, I still have depression and PTSD, are they laughing because of that? NO! I AM SORRY!! BUT PLEASE DON'T LAUGH AT ME!!" Mara got scared, and started shivering, "You are suspended! What why?" "Threatening" Mara started crying, "Please! Leave me! That was the past! Why am I getting flashbacks of it? It's like a hallucination! Eric? Help me!" Mara got scared, she heard laughs, "AAAAHHH!! STOP LAUGHING" She covered her ears and fell, "You are a failure!" "You are weird" "All doing for some attention!" "You are wrong!" Mara couldn't stop her tears, it was very painful for her... "Look at this steel bottle!" "Were you always this angry?" "Nobody likes you!" "All because of you!" "You did this to yourself!" Those were the words she kept thinking, she started feeling a headache.

A few minutes later, "Mara! Mara! Wake up!" Eric tried to wake Mara, and she woke up, "Water for you," Eric said. She drank the water, "What happened to me? I felt like I was getting hallucinated" Mara said, "I am sorry" Eric said, "Sorry? For what are you sorry?" Mara was confused, "This all happened because Nia started laughing, it was familiar for you, and you started having flashbacks, it was very painful, right? I was watching, I was crying, but couldn't help you, because everyone went against us! Shawn, Andy, and Kenneth, bet me, I couldn't do anything, I was lying down filled with my own blood, I wish I could help you but... Ida, Nia, and Helen, all were around you, laughing and making you remember those horrible memories" Eric said, "Don't be sorry! You already did a lot for me!" Mara said and smiled and hugged him... "Look at those eyes! They are so red!" Eric said, "It hurts..." Mara replied, "Let's grab some juice, college is over," Eric said, "Okay..." Mara said and they went to a juice shop, while they were walking, Mara called her mother...

"Hey, mom! I got another flashback... Nia did that! Yeah, I am feeling okay right now, I am trying my best to distract myself..." Mara said, "Oh my god, come home soon!" Mrs. Reia got worried, "Mom, I am heading to the juice shop, it makes me calm for some reason... And I get a chance to walk also! Don't worry about me, I feel okay now, if I think about anything else, I will forget it!" Mara said, "I hope so you forget them!" Mrs. Reia said...

CHAPTER X

The Mystery Death

A few weeks later, it was Sunday, and Mara was studying in her house, Mrs. Reia switched on the television and started seeing the news channel, "A 21-year-old girl had died in our city, and it looks like she committed suicided as she stabbed herself with a kitchen knife, the weapon was found in her hand" The news reporter said, "What? A person died in our city?" Mrs Reia was surprised, "The person's name is *Nia Micheals*" The news reporter continued, Mrs. Reia couldn't believe it, "Nia died?!" She said, "Mara! Did you know about this?" She asked, "What!?" Even Mara couldn't believe it, and she started dancing, "Did she suicide? I think the god of the underworld, Hades, took her because she did so many sins!" Mara laughed, and Mrs Reia also laughed. "Okay, happiness and jokes besides. Mom, why would she suicide? She doesn't have any reason to do it" Mara said, "Who knows? The police didn't get any suicide letter too" Mrs Reia said "She did seem happy these past weeks, it's bizarre..." Mara said.

The next day, "Mom! I am going to college!" Mara went to college happily, "Finally no one to make fun of me... No, there are still people tho!" Mara thought, "Hey!" Eric said, "So... have you done the practical?" He asked, "Yes!" Mara replied, while they were walking, they saw Ida crying, and Mara... *smiled looking at her*, she is still crying about Nia's death" Eric said. "Why would she do it!?" Ida screamed, everyone was giving their sympathy to her but, Eric and Mara looked at her, having no pity, "That's karma! When I was screaming, in terrible pain, *they were laughing at me.*

And now, *I will smile!*" Mara said happily, "Karma!" Eric said.

Later, Ida went to her house, "Police came here, you should go to the police station" Mrs Jameson said, "Okay mom..." Ida replied, she was feeling tired, and her eyes were red like blood. She went to the police station, "You wanted to see me?" Ida asked tiredly, "Yes, about Nia's death," The police officer, Derek Lake said, Ida couldn't believe it, she wasn't feeling well, "I am telling you! That girl is not Nia, she is someone else!" Ida became mad. "Miss. Jameson, haven't you seen her dead body? It's her!" Officer Lake tried to explain to her, "NO! NO!" Ida started crying, officer Lake tried to calm her, but a few minutes later, she remained silent, "Now, Miss. Jameson, do you think Nia was having suicidal thoughts?" He asked, "Of course not! She was a happy girl, no one bullied her, she didn't have any mental illness, and she can't suicide!" Ida explained, "Then, why would she suicide?" Her death was a mystery...

Mara and Eric were happy today, "I was having so much pressure! So many were there to bully and trouble me. Now that Nia is dead, I think it reduced to 10%" Mara said to Eric, "10%?" Eric asked with a confused face. Mara and Eric talked for a while and went to their class...

The next day; DAY 2- The investigation into Nia's death was still going, police officers were busy searching for evidence of her mysterious death. "Did you get any evidence?" Officer Lake asked, "No..." Another officer said. They found themselves at a dead end... "Have you checked all the rooms?" Officer Lake asked, "We completely checked the living room, the place where she died," The other officer said, "Okay. Then, I will check other rooms" Officer Lake said and went inside Nia's house. He went to check Nia's bedroom, he looked around and said, "It's weird, all photos are without Ida or any other person, aren't they best friends? All photos are just her! Whatever... who am I to judge her?" Then, he went to the kitchen and, *found a piece of evidence*, "What are these?" He asked himself and picked up the evidence, they were some kind of pills, Derek didn't have any knowledge about medicines or pills, "But, I know a person who knows of this! My fiancée!" Officer Lake said to himself, he put the pills in a zip lock bag, and going outside to his other partners, "Any luck?" They asked, "Yep! I found these pills on the kitchen floor!" Officer Lake showed the pills. "You should show this to Sandra!" The officer said, "Yes, that's what I was thinking, I will go to her place and see what is these pills..." Officer Lake said. And he went to the therapist.

"Sandra?" Officer Lake asked, "What happen, officer Lake?" Dr May asked, "You can call me Derek!" Officer Lake said, Dr. May smiled, "What brings you here? You got any evidence?" Dr Maya asked, "Yes, I found these pills in her house" Officer Lake gave the pills to Dr May, "Hmm... wait a few minutes, I will just examine and come," Dr May said and went with the pills. A few minutes later, she came back, "So, what are these?" Officer Lake asked, "Are you sure Nia was not depressed?" Dr May asked, "Yes, Ida told me," Officer Lake said, "Honey, these are Antidepressant pills! They are used to treat the major depressive disorder, anxiety disorders, and other things. This means Nia was suffering from depression or anxiety" Dr May said, "What?!" Officer Lake was very confused, "But Ida said Nia was not suffering from anything" "There are many possibilities, either Nia was suffering but Ida didn't know about it or she knew but didn't tell, or any other reason," Dr May said, "I should ask her again," Officer Lake said. He went to Ida's house,

He knocked on the door, and Ida came to open the door, "Officer?" She asked, "Miss. Jameson, I have a question, was Nia suffering from depression or anything?" Officer Lake asked her, "You have asked already... NO! She was not suffering!" Ida said angrily, "But I found these in her house," Officer Lake said and showed the antidepressant pills. Ida was completely blank, "No! This can't be! She never had depression" Ida couldn't believe it. *Nia had depression and that's why she committed suicide. Case Closed. But why did she had depression? Only Nia knows*

CHAPTER XI

Fake Friend: Nia Micheals

The college ended, "Hey, Eric? Ever since I told my mother about you, she wants to meet you, so I was thinking to invite to my house, will you come?" Mara said to Eric, "Oh! Sure, I would love to meet Mrs Reia" Eric said happily, "Mom is waiting for this day!" Mara said. She took Eric to her house, they went inside, "Mom! Look who I bought with me?" Mara said, Mrs. Reia came, "Eric? Nice to meet you!" Mrs Reia smiled, "Hi, Mrs Reia" Eric said politely, "I have heard many things about you" Eric looked at Mara, "Anyways, I made some snacks for you, just wait," Mrs Reia said and went to the kitchen. "Mrs Reia is very humble," Eric said to Mara... "Mara, mind if I switch on the television?" He asked, "Not at all, think it is as your own home" Mara replied, he switched on the television and they started to watch the news channel.

"It's been two days since Miss. Micheals's death. Finally, today officer Derek Lake found the reason behind her death. Officer Derek found antidepressant pills in Nia's house, which only means Nia was mentally-ill and since in most cases, depression ends by taking our own life, maybe Nia was one of them. She committed suicide to end her depression" The news reporter said, Eric and Mara were confused, "What the" "This is bullcrap! How the hell she was mentally ill and suffering from depression?" Mara was confused. "What's the matter, dear?" Mrs. Reia came, "Mom, look! Nia, depression? these aren't even close? How can a girl like Nia get depression? She gave others depression!" Mara said angrily, "Mara, look!" Eric said, Mara looked at the television, "I feel pity for her..." "She didn't deserve it," Some citizens said, Mara was shocked after hearing it, "Pity?! Ask them who she bullied! She didn't feel pity for them... She did deserve that!" Mara was raged...

"Now let's talk with Nia's bestfriend..." After hearing this, Mara burst into laughing, Eric and Mrs. Reia were confused, "Why are you laughing?" They asked, "Bestfriend?" Mara smiled... "She was my best friend... Why did god take it away from me?! I just can't accept the truth that SHE DIED!! I was with her for 4 years, and we knew each other, I don't know how I didn't know about her depression. She was a happy girl, but left me as a sad girl" Ida said and tears dropped from her eyes. But, Mara couldn't stop her laugh, "Ida still thinks of her as her best friend! But the truth is, Nia never had any best friends! Even I thought the same things about Nia! But, she just loves bullying and betraying her friends!" Mara explained why she was laughing.

Mara was smiling, but suddenly it faded away, "YOU ARE A LOSER!!" She started hearing the voices of Nia, Mara got scared and started shaking, and Eric saw her, "Mara, you alright?" He asked, she started crying, "Mara!?" He shouted, she closed her eyes and ears, "Mara! Mara!" Eric now understood, she was having flashbacks, "We are best friends forever!" Said Nia from 2009, "AAAHH!!" Mara shouted, "You can't ask questions!" "Mara, I know what I did to you in middle school, but that doesn't mean we can't be friends. I apologize, I am sorry" She kept hearing these things... Mrs. Reia came, "Mara!" She went to her and hugged her, "Dear, you okay?" Mara was still shaking. A few minutes later, Mara opened her eyes, "Water for you" Eric gave her the glass bottle, She drank water... She looked sad and then, tears dropped from her eyes, Mrs. Reia wiped her tears, "Mom, why am I doing this to myself?" Mara asked, looking at Mrs. Reia, "You still wouldn't stop blaming yourself?" Mrs. Reia asked, "You did nothing!" "I did! I was the one who started talking about my past, that's why I remembered it, that's why I got those flashbacks!" Mara said sadly...

The next day, Eric came to pick up Mara, he knocked on the door, and Mrs. Reia came to open it, "Eric?" She asked, "What are you doing here?" "Oh, today I thought to go college with Mara. So, I am here to pick her up" Eric said, "Oh, that's nice! Mara will be here soon" Mrs. Reia said. A few minutes later, Mara came to the door, "Hi..." She said, Hey..." Eric replied and they went to college, while walking, Mara asked Eric, "Why do you come to pick me up?" "To talk with you. How are you feeling today?" Eric asked, "Better than yesterday" Mara replied, "Don't think about that much" Eric said, "You talked with Mrs. Reia?" "Yeah, after you left, I talked with mom, and felt better..." Mara replied. "Good to hear," Eric said.

They reached college and went to their class... After their class ended, they went to sit outside to take some fresh air, and talked for a while, smiling and laughing... A few minutes later, Ida came outside too, she saw Eric and Mara happy, so she got angry and went towards them, "You guys look very happy! Aren't you sad!?" She asked, Eric and Mara, looked at them each other, and they were confused, "Why should we be sad?" Eric asked, "Nia is dead!! You are not sad for her!?" Ida asked, "Why should we feel sad for someone like her? She made my life hell!" Mara said, "What? No, she did not!" Ida said, "What do you know about her? You have been friends with her for just 4 years! I have been with her since 2009! That's like 13 years! She didn't make my life hell, you say? Then explain how she bullied me and broke our friendship of ours. Nia told me the same lies she told you, we will be always together blah blah! Just after 3 years, she betrayed me. She became my friend, get to know my secrets, and exposed them, whole class laughed at me, I was humiliated, got traumatized, and suffered from depression and PTSD, lived painfully for these 13 years! Not only she did do these things to me but to other innocent children, she befriended 4 or more children, and did the same process, befriend, know secrets, expose, betray and bully! She doesn't even know how it feels to those innocent children! Once she gets bored, she chooses another prey! You are one of them! That's why she befriend you! You and Nia would bully me because she liked but once she gets bored, she will humiliate you too! She will betray and bully you. Then, there's no difference between you and me. Luckily, you didn't have to see those days since she died! So, instead of crying on her death, be thankful that you were saved from being her prey!" Mara said, everyone stopped to hear it, Ida was shocked to hear Nia's past, "What... Nia is such a type of person? But, I thought she is a kind friend" Ida said, "That's what I thought and look what happened to me" Mara said. "Whatever, she was kind to me, and I will miss her," Ida said and went away, "What the hell!? After hearing your paragraph, she is still sad for her?!" Eric was confused, "Let her be, I warned her, that's her problem" Mara replied.

CHAPTER XII

Depression: Ida Jameson

Ida sat on a bench, "I should go home..." She thought. She went home and started thinking, "Maybe she was not the wrong person" Everyone has a perspective, either they see it from a wrong perspective or a good one, Ida thought Nia was a good person because she never saw the truth after all, *action speaks louder than words.* Soon, everything felt weird, "Mara, have you seen Ida?" Eric asked, "No, she is missing classes" Mara replied. That was true, Ida stopped coming to college... At night, Ida couldn't get enough sleep, "Ida? You okay?" Mrs Jameson asked her, "I couldn't sleep, mom" Ida replied, it happened for many days, "GOD!! I JUST WANT TO SLEEP!!" She started shouting, and Mrs Jameson was scared. One day Ida decided to go to the pharmacy, "Hey, I need pills for insomnia" Ida said, "These are Antidepressants, Benzodiazepines, and some other drugs" Dr May said... "Thanks," Ida said and took the drugs and went away... Before sleeping she would take the pills and tries to sleep, luckily, she started to sleep 8 hours like a normal person. But that doesn't mean her depression has been treated, she is still stressed about it, and tried therapy, but still didn't feel any better.

One day, a tragedy happened... "Officer Lake!! There's another death!!" Said an officer, they went to the person's death, and Dr May sighed, "She died due to overdose..." She said, "My god!" Said officer Jason Holland, Derek's partner. Officer Lake stared at the body, "Name: *Ida Jameson*, Age: 21 years old, Gender: Female..." Dr May was writing, Officer Lake looked at the pills, "Overdose, indeed' He said to himself.

"Mara, did you know how to do the last practical? I couldn't understand" Eric said to Mara, "Don't worry, I will tell you in the hospital" Mara replied, they went to the college, they looked around, all were sad, "What's going on?" Mara asked, suddenly, Norman came in front of them, "Ida was found dead this morning!" He said, "What!?" Eric was shocked, but, Mara wasn't, "Yeah... she died due to overdose, after all, she had depression" Norman continued, "Depression? How did that happen?" Mara asked, "Oh, she was still sad about Nia's death" Norman replied, "Wow! That idiot died two weeks ago, and her idiot 'friend' died too, for being sad for her" Mara said sarcastically, "Aren't you both sad for her?" Norman asked, "Why should I? I don't even know her well" Eric said, "Yeah, why should I feel sad for someone who used me?" Mara said. Both didn't seem to care much about Nia, instead, they were busy doing the practicals...

"These drugs... Antidepressants, Benzodiazepines, honey these are pills for insomnia. And I even remember giving to her..." Dr May said to Officer Lake, "Yes, Miss. Jameson suffered from insomnia, Mrs Jameson said... "So, are we going to do anything?" Dr May asked, "Nah, our investigation is already over. I mean, what are we supposed to do? We know the reason, we know how it happened. Our job is done" Officer Lake said, "Jason is busy talking with Mrs Jameson, after their talk, we will go" He continued. Mrs Jameson was still shocked at what happened to her daughter, "Mrs Jameson, what do you think about it?" Officer Holland asked, "If she would have not thought about that Nia, maybe she wouldn't have to see this..." Mrs Jameson, "Okay... take care, Mrs Jameson," Officer Holland said awkwardly and went to officer Lake and Dr May,

"Investigation over, and so our job here," Officer Holland said and the three went away...

The college ended, and Mara went back home, "So, I heard about Ida" Mrs Reia said, "You did? It came on television too" Mara said uninteresting, "By your look, I can say, something is not right, what happened?" Mrs Reia said. "Today, in the college, all just asked me about... Ida! I wasn't even her friend! Thank god she died!" Mara said, "Oh... just as I thought, you are not at all sad for her," Mrs. Reia said, "Mom, I never feel pity for someone who is filled with sins," Mara said.

CHAPTER XIII

They are a sinner to me

The next day, Mara got ready and went to the college, "Eric, completed the practical?" Mara asked, "Yeah, thanks for the help you did yesterday!" Eric said and smiled, "No problem" Mara replied. As usual break time, Eric and Mara went outside and talked... no sooner, someone came towards them, "Hey..." That voice, it was familiar, Mara looked at the person and was shocked, "What the hell are you doing!?" Eric said angrily, *Helen smiled.* "Haven't I told you to never talk with us?!" Mara said staring at her, "Haven't you told me you wouldn't care? After all, I am not talking to you" Helen said, Mara was silenced, "So, Eric, how are you?" She continued talking with Eric, meanwhile, Mara was silent and staring at both of them, "GO AWAY!" Eric said angrily. "To be honest, I want some fun... Boys! Make him remember that day!" Helen called Shawn, Andy, and Kenneth, Eric was confused, "Hey! H-HEY! What the hell did I Do?!" He asked, "Since Nia and Ida had left me, I will continue to do what they wanted, after all, *we have the same enemy.* Mara saw the three, with bats and weapons, "HELEN!! Your enemy is me, not Eric! He did nothing!" Mara said, "Eric is no different than you," Helen said, "I really thought you don't come to college for studying, but now it has been proven too!" Mara said. "ERIC RUN!!" Mara screamed, "Guys, we can defeat Mara mentally..." Helen said to them. Before Eric could run, Shawn and Andy captured him and took him somewhere, "Mara, do you remember this?" Kenneth said, showing a steel bottle, Mara started shaking, and she started to have flashbacks,

"NOO!!!!" She started screaming, and Helen and Kenneth laughed. Unfortunately, they left no mercy to Eric, Shawn and Andy bet him so hard, they wouldn't stop until they wanted to, Eric's face, the whole body, it was like he was showering with his blood, the clothes, just covered with redness, after one hour of continues beatings, they decided they would stop and left him there... What did Eric do wrong? That was Eric's question.

After hours, Mara was conscious, she drank water from her glass bottle, and went to find Eric, he was in the college's store room, "ERIC!!" She came running to him, she couldn't see him like that, and couldn't stop crying, she took Eric to a hospital, and he was admitted, Mara was scared, a few minutes later, after waiting impatiently, she saw the doctor coming, "Do-Doctor, how's Eric?" Mara said, "Those injuries, they will take some days, maybe weeks to recover" The doctor replied, Mara became sad, and she went to Eric's room, "Eric!?" She looked as if she was going to cry, "Mara" Eric tried his best to smile, "What did they do to you?" She said sadly, "That was sudden, why would they do it?" Eric was still confused, Mara sighed and said, "Because, she was Nia and Ida's friend. And everyone wanted to bully us, and today, they just took it far!" Mara said, "So, this was bullying!? This is what we call half murder!" Eric replied, "Don't worry, Eric. I am gonna take revenge for you... Not only they abused us physically, but mentally too! But I am also gonna do worst than this" Mara said with an evil laugh, Eric got scared, "Hey, what are you gonna do?" He said, "Don't worry, take care, see you later?" Mara said and smiled.

The next day, "Hi, Helen..." Mara said staring at Helen, What the hell do you want?" Helen said annoyed, "Oh, I don't want anything I am here to give you a warning,"

Mara said and smiled, "What warning? That you exist?" Helen asked, "Oh wow! Yes, your guess is correct!" Mara said and went away, "What does she think herself?" Helen went to her class, and being Helen, she didn't focus on the class and looked around the class, half an hour later, she went outside of the class, "The class is boring!" She said to herself. "I should find the boys..." She went on a walk to find the three, but she couldn't find them... "It will be very weird, but let's check the store room too" She went to the store room and found the three tied up with rope and their whole body was covered with blood, "SHAWN! ANDY! KENNETH!" She shouted and opened them, "How did this happen?" She was very scared, "You should look behind..." They said, Helen was already scared, after hearing that, she got more scared, slowly she turned back, click! That was the sound they heard, Mara started laughing, she was behind them with a cell phone, "Look at this scared face! Now let's post this to your social media!" Mara said, "My phone!?" She checked herself, "I took it when you weren't looking around, look they are started to even have comments" Helen snatched the phone from her and saw the comments, "Look at her face!" "Scared cat!" All were making fun of her, "Don't worry, that blood is not real, it's just red paint. *I don't do violence like you all*" Mara said. They came outside, and the class had already ended... "I saw your face!" People started to make fun of Helen, "AAAH!! STOP!!" She begged, "So, how does it feel tasting your own medicine?" Mara smiled and went away,

she looked at the three, "Three sinners" She told herself, "Hey! Where are you going?" She asked, "Ugh..." They were too scared, "You know, I can tell the principal of our college about Eric's truth, as I am a witness, there's a chance they would believe me because you guys are so disgusting, wouldn't even wash your bats? This means you can get expelled, and your career of being a Radiologist, a Neurologist, and a Cardiologist are... DEAD! So, I will never be like Nia and be a snitch, so I will just give you a warning, and things get worse, remember these words" Mara threatened them. "Oh-okay," They said nervously and went away... And, Mara went to her class too.

In the evening, Mara went to the hospital, "Hey, Eric! How are you feeling today, fine?" Mara asked, "Yeah! Of course, I mean those three came to me and apologized! What did you do?" Eric was confused, "Oh, nothing some threats and pranks!" Mara said, "Oh..." Eric was silenced, "Don't worry, I did nothing violent!" Mara said. And, they both continued talking...

CHAPTER XIV

He is back...why?

A month later, finally, Eric was cured and was able to go back to college, "I can't wait to go back to college! I wonder if I missed anything?" Eric asked, Mara, smiled and replied, "You didn't miss anything!" They reached college and went to attend their class, "Hey, Eric! How are you feeling now?" The professor asked, "I am feeling much better" Eric replied, "What happened to you?" The professor seemed curious, "I was in an accident" Eric said, "Oh... how bad" The professor replied and continued his lecture...

The class ended, and Mara and Eric went to take some fresh air... "Hi..." Comes another annoying person, "What do you want?" Mara asked in an annoying mood, "Nothing..." He said, "Norman, what? you didn't get any other girl so you just came to Mara?" Eric asked, Mara, ignored Norman and went, "Hey, where are you going?" Norman asked, Mara, didn't care and went... "You can't go like this!" Norman said to himself.

At lunchtime, he came back, Eric was right, I mean what does he do in the college, just harasses girls... He tried his best to come closer to Mara, but he failed, "Time to change the prey" He decided. And started to go to other girls, Mara wasn't like normal girls who would be helpless in situations like this, those girls are easy for him...

Before college ended, an incident happened, blood was there on the ground, "What happened here?" Mara asked others, "A girl jumped from the third floor, reason, nobody knows," A person said to her, she was shocked, "Who was she? What was her name?" "Martha Gorman" The reply came, "That's the girl whom Norman was roaming around... the class has ended, she ran to the anesthesiology class, Eric too came with her, "What are you doing here?" Eric asked, "Trying to find Martha's bench, hey look, a paper, not suspicious," Mara said and took the paper and started reading,

"Someone help me, please! Someone read this message, I am too scared to tell. But, Norman Spencer, kept on harassing me, touching me inappropriately, and after taking me to the store room and doing that to me, I have no will to live now... So, I have decided to go to the third floor and end my life.

-Martha Gorman"

Mara and Eric were shocked after reading it. "To be honest, I saw that girl around Norman, I decided to find that- because he was not even in the crowd... But, he was not even in this class, anyways, I found this, now I can jail him!" Mara said and went outside of the college, "Hey, are you going to the police station?" Eric asked, "Of course, what do you think?" Mara replied. Eric was speechless.

"Hey! I am here to file a complaint against a rapist!" Mara said, "What's the matter, little sister?" Officer Lake asked, "Officer, your colleagues have gone to an investigation on the body at V.K Medical College, Suicide, reason, I have," Mara said and put the suicide letter on the table, "Officer, this is the suicide letter by the victim, Martha Gorman, you can even see, her signature, just read!" Officer Lake took the letter and started reading it, "Who's Norman Spencer?" He asked, "That rapist! Because of him, she suicides!" Mara said, "Good, little sister" Officer Lake, "We will talk with him" "You better be, Officer" Mara replied, and they went out of the police station, Eric couldn't control his smile, "What was that?" "Giving justice to someone who didn't deserve death" Mara too smiled.

"You heard what she said? Let's find that guy!" Officer Lake said and went to the college, the principal came to them, "Officer, do you need any help?" He asked, "Oh, sir, I would love to. I am here to find a student named Norman Spencer" Officer Lake said, "I guess he went to his house" The principal said, "Then I need his address" Officer Lake, "I will give officer but, what's the matter?" "Oh, your student raped another student" After hearing this, the principal was shocked. "Thank you for the address!" Officer Lake smiled, "He should be behind those cells!" The principal said angrily...

The police burst into Norman's house, "This is the police!" They found Norman, "Oh, look who is hiding like a rat!?" Officer Lake said Norman was arrested for rape. Then, he was expelled from the college too, "So, why did you rape that poor girl?" Officer Lake asked, "Because I like to" Norman answered, "Wow! You are truly a piece of crap! Harassing and raping innocent girls just because you like to? That's the lamest and bullcrap reason I have ever heard in my life!" Officer Lake was pissed off and even started to hate Norman...

"That's what I wanted! May rest in peace, although I never knew you" Mara said. But, when Mr Spencer knew about his son getting arrested, he wasn't happy about it, "What is this son?" He asked, "Whatever, I am going to bail you out," He said. And just after living in jail for a day, he was bailed out, but never was found again, they never saw him again... "He is free..." Eric said to Mara, "Why?" She asked...

CHAPTER XV

Fell in death

A few weeks later, people stopped caring about Helen, they wouldn't even talk to her, and she felt lonely there... She went to her home, "Hi, dad..." She said, "I need your help, do some work," Mr. Robins said, "Yeah, I will make the chair," Helen said, "She doesn't work. I doubt she studies in college too" Mrs. Robins said to Mr. Robin. Helen had bad relationships with her parents, they think of her as a disappointment they have made.

Helen took the woods and saw, "Daughter" Mr. Robins came, "What happened, dad?" She asked, "Ugh, actually this order is to be done by tomorrow morning, so it would be better if you work night too, after all, you are a night owl" Mr. Robins smiled and went, "Okay, dad," Helen said. She started cutting and shaping the chairs... "I am their worker..." Helen said to herself, "When did you start talking to yourself?" The voice came, Helen looked behind and saw her mother, "What are you doing here?" She asked, "I was here to take the nails" She took the nails from the shelf, "Helen, what do you think?" Mrs. Robins asked, "What do you mean?" Helen was confused, "Worker? You think we would treat you like a princess, but the world is not like that! *The world will never treat you how you want*, nor we will. What do you think? We would not know what you will do in college. Attract people, want some attention, and be in fights? You don't go to college to study, right? If it continued, you are never going to get a degree, so just help your father" Mrs. Robins said. "And what would you do? Make your daughter-" Mrs. Robins got angry, and she slapped Helen, "Just try to understand what I mean!" She said angrily, "You have to work to earn anything!" And she went with the nails. Helen went back to her work...

By the evening, she completed three chairs, "More three to do" She said to herself and started working, it was 11 PM, and she finally completed making the six chairs, "Everything is done" She said and smiled. And kept all the things in their place, the hammer and nails on the shelf, the wood by the wall, she took the chairs and kept them in her father's workplace. "Here you go dad, all chairs are done," She said, "Good job, daughter" Mr. Robins replied. She went back to her workplace and sat at her desk and started watching her cell phone, suddenly, Mrs. Robins came, "Helen, it's 11 PM, it would be better if you sleep now" She said, "Ok mom, I will" Helen replied, but, she didn't listen and continued watching cell phone...

The next day, it was 7 AM, "The orders have been sent to the owner, by afternoon, they will get it" Mr. Robins said to Mrs. Robins, "Hey, where is Helen?" He asked, "Probably sleeping, I will wake her up," Mrs. Robins said and went to Helen's room, but she was not there, "Maybe she slept in her workplace?" And went to her workplace only to see *she is in permanently sleeping,* Helen was laying on the ground, blood coming from her head and the floor was filled with redness along with a hammer with blood stains. "HELEN!!" Mrs. Robins shouted and took Helen in her arms, *she was dead,* Mr. Robins came to see the matter, he was shocked and took his cell phone and called the police.

Officer Lake came to investigate along with his partners, "Officer, what happened to our daughter?" Mr. and Mrs. Robins asked, "Sir and ma'am, please wait, we are trying to find it" Officer Lake tried to calm them, officer Lake looked at the hammer, he wore his gloves, and took the hammer,

"Blood in the hammer," He said and looked at the floor and said, "Blood in the floor" "We need to test them out, honey, examine and see," He said to Dr. May and gave the hammer to her. A few minutes later, Dr. May came to him, she seemed sad, "Blood on the floor, blood in the hammer, and Miss. Robins's blood, all are the same" She said, "What does this mean?" Mr. and Mrs. Robins asked, "It means only one thing, *Miss. Robins was injured with this hammer*" Officer Lake said, "Sir and ma'am, do you have any idea where this hammer could have been?" "I know, it will be on that shelf," Mrs. Robins said, pointing to the shelf which is right above Helen's desk. Officer Lake was shocked to hear it, "It only means one thing... *Miss. Robins's death was an accident*" He said, "How!?" Mr. and Mrs. Robins asked, "That hammer would have fallen from the shelf and smashed Miss. Robins's head and she died, it can be possible by the distance between them" Officer Lake explained. Mr. and Mrs. Robins couldn't stop crying.

It was 8 AM, "Mom, I am going to college," Mara said, she noticed Mrs. Reia wasn't paying attention, "Mom?" She asked, "Sorry, what were you saying?" Mrs. Reia asked, "You are always watching television," Mara said with an unamused face, "Look at the television yourself," Mrs. Reia said, Mara, looked at the television, "Another day, another death... This morning a couple of named Robins reported that their daughter, Helen Robins died in an accident, a hammer fell and smashed her head leading to her tragic death" The news reporter said, Mara was shocked, "WHAT!!" "The worst way to die" Mrs. Reia sadly, Mara couldn't believe that Helen died, although she was not sad for her, it was weird for her... She was confused and went to college... "Eric! You heard the news?" Mara asked, "Yeah! Her death was like one in a million chance!" Eric replied.

Both talked about it for a while and they went back to studying...

In the meantime, Shawn was roaming with her girlfriend, Shelby Smith, "So, I was thinking we can hang out sometime" Shawn said, "There's something I wanted to say" Shelby said, "I know, it's been 11 months, next month is our anniversary but, to be honest, *I don't want this relationship.* So, I just want a breakup" She said, Shawn was surprised, but Shawn, what can he even do? So, he accepted the breakup and Shelby left him, "It's gonna be fine" Shawn said to himself, and tried not to cry, "Hey man!"Andy and Kenneth came to him, "What happened? You look sad" Andy asked, "Nothing, Shelby left me," Shawn said sadly, "What!? Hey man, it's okay, don't feel too sad, we are here for you" Kenneth said. Shawn smiled, "What's up with you two?" He asked, "Well, I am too have some bad news, I just don't feel like living, it feels like I am under stress and pressure like everyone just wants me to become a Neurologist and, I am not doing this for myself, but for other's desire," Andy said, "Andy, don't feel like that" Kenneth said, "What about you?" Shawn asked Kenneth, "I have good news! So, my family is having a small party kind of thing in our house, and you both are invited! But it's next month..." Kenneth said happily, "Really? We would love to come, no problem we can wait a month" Shawn and Andy replied, the three talked about the party and planned many things...

CHAPTER XVI

Suicide was the only option

A week later, Shawn went to a shop, "Hey, can I get these ropes" He asked, "Ugh, sure" Said the cashier, he bought them and went home... took a piece of paper, and started writing, he wiped his tears,

"I just wanted to be happy, but guess everything feels broken after the heart breaks... I made a mistake to love someone who never loved me back. After that day, I faked my smiles, faked my happiness, and... made fool of everyone. Now, I will apologize to everyone, mom, dad, I am sorry, I never was a good son, Andy, and Kenneth, sorry for making a fool of you, and apologies to everyone. Nothing feels like those normal days, I am trying my best to be strong, but how can we fix this heart? I don't have the happiness to fix it, so I am gonna risk my life for this, sorry Kenneth, but I wouldn't be able to come to your picnic. And, whoever will be able to read this, don't make a mistake like me which I am gonna make, there are many things than this, enjoy your life forever, and love yourself"

-Shawn Verne

"Why am I even doing this?" Shawn asked himself... He took the rope and stared at it. It was evening, and Mrs Verne was worried about Shawn being in his room for too long, "Where's Shawn? I am going to check on him" She said to Mr Verne and went to his room, she was shocked, "SHAWN!!" *Shawn had hanged himself to death.* Mrs Verne couldn't stop crying, she looked at his desk and saw a piece of paper, "What is this?" She asked, it was his suicide letter, and after reading it, she wailed more... After his breakup with Shelby, he couldn't find happiness and took this harsh step, May he rest in peace

The next day, Andy and Kenneth were sitting on the bench, and tried to stop their tears, "WHY!! Did he leave us?" Kenneth cried Andy hugged him, even though he can't stop crying... they wiped their tears, and walk away... "I feel bad for them," Eric said looking at them, "Yeah... still they are sinners for me, but losing a friend is way more hurtful than any other physical pain" Mara replied.

A few weeks later, Andy looked at their picture, "Look at this picture of ourselves, Shawn you looked so happy, why did you leave? I just can't believe it's been eleven days... it always feels like yesterday. Look at my face, I look so sad" Andy said to himself and cried... he took a piece of paper and wrote something... and highlighted some words, and went home. Took a sharp pen and... "Andy, where are you? I have called you like hundred times!" Mrs Maltin shouted, she came to Andy's house, and her eyes were wide open, "Andy!?" She shouted and saw her son, *he was dead, he killed himself with that sharp pen.* She was in absolute pain, she saw a piece of paper lying down, and read...

"I read in the book, the continuous physical force exerted on or against an object by something in contact with it is called **pressure**. Then, I saw the television, **itwas** showing a lion **killing** its prey. Then, I saw another thing, I didn't understand, what was its **me**aning? Then, I met my friend who was **from** another state, he came **inside** my home and we talked."

Some words were highlighted, and she read them too, "Pressure. It was killing me from inside" She was left crying... The pressure Andy talked about, he wasn't able to take it, he was not feeling like himself, he couldn't take it and end by ending his own life.

The next day, after Kenneth heard the news, he went to the same bench where they always usually sit, "You both are the worst and best friends! You left and went!?" Kenneth was struggling to even speak, and took a deep breath but continued crying, "And... you both are liars! You said you will come to my party! But" Kenneth bite his lips and tries to continue, but he couldn't. He closes his eyes and tries to be calm... And opened his eyes, stood up, and went away... It is hard time for Kenneth to lose two friends.

A few days later, it was Sunday, the day Kenneth's small party will happen. Everyone was preparing for it, "Kenneth, set up the table" Mrs Foster said, "Okay mom" Kenneth replied, he took the cloth and put it on the table... After so much preparation, they were ready for the party, "It would have been better if Shawn and Andy had joined" Kenneth said sadly, everyone felt sad... After eating, everyone was enjoying themselves. Kenneth went to his room and lay in his bed, "I thought this party would be fun, but it's just..." He said. Suddenly, downstairs, everyone started shouting, Kenneth heard it, and tried to go downstairs, he tries to open the door but, it was locked, "Why is not opening?" He asked, and tries to open it, but he wasn't able to... and then, he saw fire and understood, *his house was on fire*, the fire raised and his whole room was on fire, and he was in between them. Soon, a firetruck came to his house, and the firemen saved everyone but Kenneth was not to be seen, "Where's Kenneth!?" Mr Foster asked, unfortunately, the firemen couldn't save Kenneth and *he burned to death*, they saw his burned body, "KENNETH!!!" Mr and Mrs. Foster shouted, their voices cracked, they cried in pain and couldn't stop it, "Our son!" They saw their son's face, and they kept on crying, This party would be fun, but it was just a disaster and one of the most depressing nights for the

Fosters.

Like his other friends, even Kenneth left, no longer there are the three sinners... Shawn and Andy took a difficult step to end their sadness and problems, while Kenneth's death was an accident, did they deserve it? It depends on your perspective. After knowing the three sinners' death, everyone was sad, even Eric and Mara, but always, Shawn, Andy, and Kenneth will be the three sinners for Mara, she wouldn't forget what they did for her and Eric, so, even though she is sad for them, still thinks they deserved it. May they rest in peace.

CHAPTER XVII

Are these deaths connected?

Two weeks, it has been two weeks since the last death. It seems everyone has forgotten about it, but not Mara, she remembered every single death and tries not to think about it, "It's been six deaths past these four months, this city has become a sad city, either dying by suicide, or by any natural cause or it's just an accident..." Mara thought, she took her notes and started to write, but soon she stopped, "I wonder who will be the next person to die?" She thought and starts overthinking, soon she realized it, and went back to writing her notes.

Meanwhile, Eric was too studying and felt very sleepy, "I better take some caffeine," He said, and went to his kitchen, and saw there is no coffee left, "Really?" He sighed "Guess I have to go outside and buy them," He said, and took his wallet and went outside to a convenience store, "Now that I have come in the store, let's buy some groceries too!" Eric said to himself.

In the meantime, Norman was getting ready, looked at himself in the mirror and went out of his house, and headed towards a restaurant, he sat and saw a girl, he stared at her and decided to make her his prey, and went to the girl and tries to flirt with her, but she wasn't impressed and then, he started harassing her, and like every other girl, she was too scared to even report or tell nearby people. When Norman found it boring, he decided to go back home. So, he stood up and went outside the restaurant, while on his way home, something unexpected happened, he was passing by a building under construction, and suddenly unexpectedly *a steel bar fell from the building and fell on Norman*, no worker intended in doing that *it was an accident*. The workers looked down and saw Norman lying, blood coming from his head and the steel bar was nearby him. Everyone came to check on him, *he was dead...*

Eric finally completed his shopping and went outside of the store and saw a crowd, "What's going on?" He asked himself and went towards the crowd, and saw Norman's dead body, he looked at the face and... was in complete shock, "NORMAN!?" His eyes were wide open. Then he went out of the crowd and called Mara, she picked it up, "What happened?" She asked, "You need to hear this! Norman is dead!! I was coming from the store, and saw a crowd and saw his dead body!!" Eric said, "What!?" That voice was joyful, and she smiled, "That's good news for me to be honest! I mean, he was a rapist! I wished he die!" Mara said happily, "Yeah!" Eric was too happy... Now that's a deserving death! Not only was Norman harassed and raped innocent girls, but because of him, many girls' life was ruined including Martha, can't even say rest in peace to him! A real sinner!

The next day, Mara and Eric went to college happily, "Eric, I think it reduced to 100% Now there is no one to bully or make fun of us!" Mara said to Eric, "Yeah, it is happy but at the same point it is sad" Eric replied, and Mara agreed. "So, have you completed that practical?" Eric asked, "Yeah! Since I got free time, I am going on evening walks, you should too try it!" Mara replied.

Everyone felt normal for having seven deaths in just five months, something was going on, and that was Officer Lake's thinking... "How can people act normal when people are dying? Our city was not like this! No one ever committed suicide or any accidents happened!" Officer

Lake asked Dr. May, "Honey, you need to chill and stop overreacting, what do you think? Death is a very rare thing? 35,214 people die per day! So, what do you even expect?" Dr. May was pissed off, "Sandra, I didn't mean that. I mean, isn't that weird that all those victims are 21 years old? Weirder, all of them knew each other, and went to the same college too!" Officer Lake said, "So? Suicide is common in adults, especially students" Dr. May said, "You wouldn't understand, I will just tell my colleagues, and they will believe in me" Officer Lake said and went away, "Derek..." Dr. May said and got busy in seeing her appointments.

Officer Lake reached the police station, "Hey everyone" He said, "So, I was thinking that these deaths, they are connected to something! I mean, all were friends, and-" Officer Lake went in explaining, but got stopped, "Officer, we get your point that they are connected, but you can't prove them, can you?" They asked, "Yes, I can. That's why I need all your help" Officer Lake replied, "Sorry, but we can't. Because we think it is just bullcrap" They said and laughed, "C'mon man! Just accept it! They died by either suicide, natural death, or accident!" They thought the same thing which Dr. May thought, officer Lake was sad and annoyed, he thought to go back home, and went outside of the police station and found a girl,

"Hi!" The girl said, "I am Yasmine Bates" It was the same Yasmine who used to gossip about Mara... "What do you want?" Officer Lake said uninterestingly, "I heard your theory, and I believe you. Even I feel that weird" Yasmine said, hearing that officer Lake was happy, "Really?" He wanted to be sure, "Yes! Because I don't believe Nia would ever commit suicide" Yasmine said, "Wait, do you know Miss. Micheals?" Officer Lake asked, "Yes, we were fr- we knew each other" Yasmine said, in reality, she was a toady of Nia's. "So, will you help me in finding evidence to prove it?" Officer Lake asked, "Of course, then I will publish it," Yasmine said with a smile, "Publish?" Officer Lake was confused, "I am a journalist student!" Yasmine said, "Oh..." Officer Lake replied. "Officer, will you come to my house, so we can discuss it?" Yasmine asked, "Okay! I am down. I want to know the truth behind these deaths!" Officer Lake said, "Yeah, me too!" Yasmine replied. They both went to Yasmine's house...

CHAPTER XVIII

What is the truth?

Yasmine gave some water to Officer Lake. And brought a whiteboard. "So, officer do you have any conspiracy theories? Or any kind of theory?" Yasmine asked, "Not really..." Officer Lake said, Yasmine was disappointed, "Why don't we see why we feel it is connected," Yasmine said and started writing something...

Nia stabbed herself with a knife (suicide)

Ida died by overdosing (natural death)

A hammer fell on Helen (accident)

Shawn hanged himself (suicide)

Andy stabbed himself with a pen (suicide)

Kenneth burned by fire (natural death)

A steel bar fell on Norman (accident)

"Did you find anything common?" Yasmine asked, "Yeah, that they died by suicide, natural death, and accident," Officer Lake said, "Yeah... But, the order is not correct, it seems jumbled" Yasmine said, officer Lake, looked at the whiteboard for a while, "Order..." He thought. Suddenly, he noticed something, "Yasmine, look at this... a weapon, then no weapon. Knife, then no weapon, hammer, no weapon, pen, no weapon, steel bar. Very weird, right?" Officer Lake said, "Yes... I didn't notice it" Yasmine replied. "Officer, if they are connected, then something is behind them, like all deaths towards one thing, just like in movies!" Yasmine said... "Yes! We need to know it" Officer Lake replied. "All these are students of V.K medical college, why don't we talk with some students?" Yasmine asked, "We can, but we wouldn't get anything. We don't know what is that thing which is connected to all these deaths" Officer Lake said, "Yeah..." Yasmine said and bite her lips, "We just need a lead!" Officer Lake said... Suddenly, someone called Yasmine, "Hello, mom? What happened? Oh... it's tomorrow? Okay fine, tell her I will come" Yasmine said ending the call, "Officer Lake, tomorrow I am gonna be busy since my cousin's birthday is there, we will continue our investigation on Thursday," Yasmine said, "Okay," Officer Lake said and went to his home.

The next day, Yasmine got ready, she took her pocket diary and a pen, "Yasmine, are you ready?" Mrs. Bates asked, "Yes mom!" She replied, "It's gonna be boring," Yasmine said uninterestingly, "Oh it's gonna be fun! It's on the beach!" Mrs. Bates said happily, Yasmine's face was blank, "Oh..." She said. They reached the beach, the clock was pointing at 5, and everyone was busy celebrating, Yasmine found it boring and went to see the shores... "Hey, where's Yasmine?" Her cousin asked, "I don't know, she was just sitting here" Mrs. Bates said, everyone started finding Yasmine, she was nowhere to be seen, *she was missing*, they called the police, "She was just here and then, she got missing!" The police started finding her... A few minutes later, they found something, "Officer, you need to see this!" Officer Lake went to see it, and they found a dead body by the shore, after seeing the face, Officer Lake was stunned, "Yasmine!?" She got too close to the shore, didn't know too close to death too, *and drowned,* "She had died... Her heart is not beating" Dr. May said, Officer Lake was in complete surprise, *her death was natural...* "Steel bar, no weapon" Officer Lake thought, "This death is too connected!!" "Officer, look at her palm!" Officer Lake saw her palm, and something was written, "A.. ar... mur..er? *All are murders?* She is here.. and the name is erased" Officer

Lake read, "Lead! This is the lead! Honey, all these are murders! They are connected!" Officer Lake said The Bates family saw Yasmine and were in shock, and cried.

Officer Lake was too sad, but he got a lead and went to his home, "I knew something was going on! Yasmine, rest in peace... you sacrificed yourself... " Officer Lake gave his respect to Yasmine. "So all those deaths are murders, and I just need to prove them, I need to find the murderer," Officer Lake said himself, suddenly someone knocked on the door, and he opened it, it was his fiancée, "Honey, what are doing here?" He asked, "To apologize, I went opposed you, didn't believe you. Now, I saw the proof, I will support you, let's find the truth!" Dr. May said, Officer Lake smiled...

"Yasmine said these are murders, someone is behind them. *She* is here. A girl is behind them" Officer Lake said, "She killed people like a queen! No doubts, no suspicious!" Dr. May said, "Yeah, the queen of killers!" Officer Lake said, "Hey, like other killers, what if she has a nickname, KILLER QUEEN," Dr. May asked, "It would be nice. But, let's focus on investigation, shall we?" Officer Lake said. "Yasmine said me a thing yesterday, 'All these are students of V.K medical college, why don't we talk with some students?' I said, there's no point. But, since we got a lead, maybe we can get something!" Officer Lake explained, "That is a good idea, I will talk with them tomorrow," Dr. May said, a call came for officer Lake, and he talked with them, "I will come soon, I need to talk with the media, I will aware them about KILLER QUEEN," Officer Lake said and went away...

"Officer Lake! We need to know what happened to your partner, Yasmine Bates?" "She was a journalism student, curious like me. And today, she sacrificed herself and gave me a lead. These deaths! They are no suicide, natural death, or accident! ALL ARE MURDERS!! Someone is behind them, and I call her, KILLER QUEEN. She convinced us, they are just some normal deaths but truly they are murders and Yasmine was one of her victims, she made us think Yasmine died by drowning, but Killer Queen killer killed her!" All were in shock, Mara came from her evening walk and sat on the sofa, "You are seeing this?! A murderer is in our city!" Mrs. Reia said, Mara was shocked, "Murders!? Mom, our city has become too dangerous!" She said, "I hope they catch this Killer Queen soon!" Mara said angrily... "And, I, Officer Derek Lake will find and give her what she deserves!" Officer Lake took the oath, and everyone cheered...

CHAPTER XIX

Who is Killer Queen?

The next day, Dr May went to V.K medical college and asked every student she could ask, some knew them, and some didn't. Suddenly, she saw Mara, "Miss. Reia!" She called, Mara looked back, they were meeting after 5 years and were surprised, "Dr May!?" She was surprised, "What are you doing here, doc?" She asked, meanwhile, Eric was confused, "Do you know her?" He asked, "Oh yeah, she was my therapist" Mara replied, "So, how are you?" Dr May asked, "I have been good," Mara smiled, "So, do you know those victims? Nia, Ida..." "Yeah, I know them, all of them. They were the ones who bullied me!" Mara said in a serious tone, "Oh wow, you were the only one who knows all of them. What about you, little brother?" Dr May asked Eric, "I don't know all of them. I just knew about Helen, the three si- I mean, Shawn, Kenneth and Andy, and Norman, I don't know much about others" Eric replied, "I am sorry, three what?" Dr May was curious, "I and Mara call them three sinners because they nearly murdered me," Eric said, "Oh..." Dr May said and went away.

She went to officer Lake's house, "Honey, I found someone who knew all of them!" She said to him, "Oh, who is she?" He asked, "Mara Reia, she was my patient too," She said, "Oh... Then I have to talk with her" Officer Lake said... It was 3 PM, the college ended, Mara and Eric were heading to the gate, and suddenly officer Lake interrupted, "Mara Reia? Wait, I have seen you!" He said, "Yes, I came to report a file on Norman" Mara replied, "Oh yes, can you come with me, we need to talk," Officer Lake said, they went to officer Lake's house... "Miss. Reia, you seem to know all eight of them, just you! Isn't that weird? And all died, but not you" Officer Lake said, "What do you want to say? That I am Killer Queen? I killed them?" She asked, "Yes. You have reasons to, Eric said they bullied you, three sinners?" Dr May said, "You are a suspect! We don't have proof to prove them, but we are going to find them! We have eyes on you, Miss. Reia" Officer Lake said, and they let Mara go... Is Mara the killer queen?

The next day, another death was reported, officer Lake went to the victim's house, and saw a *glass vase fall on the victim, it was an accident*, "Name: *Josie Davis*, Age: 21 years old, Gender: Female..." Said officer Holland, Nia's other toady also down, "No weapon, glass vase. This is not an accident, this is another murder! By Killer Queen!" Officer Lake said... "Sandra, go ask Mara if she knows Josie" Officer lake said to Dr May, she nodded and went to Mara's house, and knocked on the door, and Mrs Reia came to open, "Hello, Natalie" Dr May smiled, "Doc? What are you doing here? After five years" Mrs Reia asked, "I came here to meet Mara" Dr May said, "Oh, lucky for you, she was just now going to college, Mara! Come here!" Mrs Reia called Mara, and she came, "Hello again, Mara," Dr May said, "So, do you know Josie Davis?" She asked, "Yes..." Mara replied, "Unfortunately, she died today, and it seems Killer Queen killed her," Dr May said, and went away... Mara too headed to college

"SHE KNOWS!!" Dr May said, "I am 100% she is the Killer Queen!" Officer Lake said, "But, we can't just arrest her, we don't have much proof, and we can't confess her too," Dr May said, "Yeah that is..." Officer Lake said, thinking for a while, "Hey, does she have any friends?" He asked, "Yeah, I think his name is Eric" Dr May replied, and officer Lake replied...

After college ended, Dr May waited for Eric, "Eric!" Dr May said, "We met yesterday!" Eric replied, "I want to ask some questions about Mara. Mara, mind if you leave us alone?" She said. Mara left them, "So, did Mara have bad relationships with all those victims?" "Yes, they all bullied them" Eric replied, "Do you think Mara is the Killer Queen?" "What!?" Eric thought for a while, "To be honest, yeah... She can do anything when she is angry" Eric replied, "Brother, will you help me? Today, you have to ask her about this. She wouldn't lie, will she? Even you want to know who is Killer Queen" Dr May asked, "Okay..." Eric replied and went to Mara, "Hey Mara, can I join you for your evening walk, I am free today" He said, "Sure" Mara replied...

In the evening, they went for the walk, "Mara, I have something to ask" Eric said in a serious tone, "No lies, tell me the truth, *are you the Killer Queen*" He finally asked, Mara, stopped, she started shaking, "How- HOW DO YOU KNOW!!??" She said angrily. So, it was true, *Mara was the Killer Queen*. Eric was shocked, he stepped back, took his cell phone, and called the police, "NO!! YOU CAN'T!!" She said, "WHY!!??" Eric asked, "I didn't know what to do!? I was blind" Mara started crying, and Eric felt sad, "Mara..." "NO!! NO ONE SHOULD KNOW ABOUT ME!!! Y-YOU CALLED POLICE!?" Mara was again angry, Eric stepped back, "YOU CAN'T DO THAT!!" Mara said, and pushed Eric, he fell into a deep hole in the right, "No one can know about me..." Mara was still shaking and started crying, soon the police came, "Miss. Mara Reia, you are under arrest" Mara looked at officer lake and her hands up, she was scared, and she got handcuffed, "Where's Eric?" She asked in a nervous tone, officer Lake took her to the hole, "There"

He pointed, and Mara was shocked, "ERIC!!!" She started crying, "What have I done?!" "Glass Vase, no weapon. You are indeed the Killer Queen" Officer Lake said, "I was so blind in killing and taking revenge, I killed nine people because of that. Eric, he did nothing wrong to me. When he asked me about Killer Queen, I had flashbacks on how killed I them, I got angry and so blind to save myself, I killed him" Mara said and cried. Officer Lake took her to the police station... Soon, everyone know who Killer Queen was, and they started to hate her, she knew it would happen, "How can I kill my friend?" She hated herself...

After living in the prison for two days, she regretted her actions... She called officer Lake, "Officer, I want one thing, can you give me?" She said, "What do you want?" He asked, "A gun" She replied, "I can't give you!" Officer Lake said, she came close to officer Lake and stole the gun, "MARA!! DON'T DO IT!!" Officer Lake warned her, she pointed to her head, "I am no different than them, I became what I hated the most and I become one of them! I am a sinner! I don't deserve to live!" She cried and pulled the trigger, "NO!!" *Mara killed herself with a gun*, "No weapon, gun" Officer Lake said...

No sooner, Mrs Reia knew about Mara's death, than she was in complete shock, she went to the police station as fast as she could and saw her daughter, her head was busted, and blood flowing like a tap. "MARA!!" She wailed and wipes her tears, Mrs. Reia was in trauma, she couldn't see her daughter like this, and went outside the police station, "The person whom I lived for... she is gone. What am I supposed to do?!" She asked herself and headed to the pharmacy, "Hey doc" She said, "Natalie, what are you doing here?" Dr May asked, "Can I get carbon monoxide?" Mrs Reia asked, "What? You are asking me a poison!" Dr May was shocked, "Just give me, doc" Mrs Reia insisted, Dr. May gave her the poison, and she drank it, "NATALIE!!" Dr May shouted, and a few minutes later, she fell, Dr. may checked her heartbeat, "It's not beating" Dr May said, *Mrs. Reia poisoned herself and died.* A sad ending...

[THE END]

Deaths And Deaths

Some of you, have guessed who Killer Queen was, but, how did she kill them without any suspicion or doubts?

18th June; it was evening, and Nia was busy doing her work, Mara break into the kitchen first, and took a knife but she didn't notice that her antidepressant pills fell down on the kitchen floor. Then, she came from Nia's window, "Hello, Nia" She said, "What are you doing here? How did you break into my house?" Nia was confused, "What did you say? I bet you can't even do that! I am here to prove you" Mara said with a smirk, Nia got scared, "What do you mean?" Her voice had fear, Mara took the knife and stabbed her since she wore gloves, there were no fingerprints of Mara on the knife, and kept the knife in Nia's hand and went away... The next day, it was reported.

You may ask how can she just come, kill and go. Remember, her evening walk?

5th July; it was evening, and Ida was still sad for Nia, suddenly, Mara came, Ida looked back, "What are you doing here?" Ida said, her voice had no power, "You are feeling sad for someone who never cared for you!" Mara said, she brought a rope too, "Aren't you going to report me? I literally break into your house!" Mara was confused, "I don't care, you want to rob me, do it," She said. Mara tied Ida and took her pills and gave all of them to Ida, she took them, and she just accepted her death, Mara was shocked herself, then untied Ida and went away... The next day, it was reported.

17th August; It was 11 PM, Mara sneaked out of her house and went to Helen's workplace, "Hi!" Mara said, "Don't try to shout!" She warned her and took the hammer from the shelf and smashed her head from it without making any noise and kept the hammer down and went away... The next day, it was reported.

26th August; Before college could end, Mara went to Shawn, "I heard about you, I feel sorry for you" Mara said to him, "Can you do some work for me?" She asked, "What?" He asked, "I know you want to die, I can do for you, but you have to write a suicide letter and buy a rope, here's the money, will you do that?" Mara asked, "I was thinking about that, okay I am down," Shawn said... In the evening, she came, "Shawn took the rope and stared at it and gave it to Mara, she took the rope and hanged Shawn, "He wished for it" Mara said to herself and went away...

6th September; Before college could end, Mara came to Andy, "Hey, I know how you feel now, don't worry everything will be fine" She said to him, "So, actually I have something to write, but I need to give due evening and I can't because I have to do some practicals to do, even Eric is with me, can you write?" Mara asked, "Sure!" Andy said, he wrote and saw the heading was highlighted, so he too highlighted the heading, and when Mara's practicals were over, he handed to her, "Thank you so much!" Mara said, then she highlighted those words and erased the heading... In the evening, she came to Andy's house, "Mara!?" He was confused, "Look at this" Mara handed a sharp pen to Andy, and he took the sharp pen and... "Today's your last day," Mara said and stabbed Andy's neck with the sharp pen, "Why do these people not report? Are they dumb?" Mara thought and went away...

18th September; it was evening, and the Fosters was enjoying themselves in the hall, Mara broke into the kitchen and switched on the stove, went upstairs quietly, closed Kenneth's room from outside, and went away from the kitchen's window, slowly the house was on fire, and Mara was looking at from a distance, burning it and smiled, and went away...

2nd October; it was evening, after studying for a while, she went for her evening walk, while walking, she saw Norman going to the restaurant and smiled. She went to the building under construction without no one noticing her and took the steel bar, she waited when Norman would come, and when he came, she dropped the steel bar and went away...

12th October; She knew about Yasmine trying to expose her, "Yasmine... you were a toady of Nia, that means I will not leave you! No one can know about me" Mara thought and went to the beach. Yasmine was seeing the shores, suddenly she saw Mara, and tries to run away, but Mara was faster than her and grabbed her and tries to drown her, she managed to write 'all are murders, she is here, Mara Reia' and Mara drowned her, by the water, some of her writing was erased, she left Yasmine in the water and went away...

13th October; After what happened to Mara, she started overthinking what officer Lake and Dr. May said to her, she was angry and wanted to end it by killing someone. She went for her evening walk and coincidently, she saw Josie in a vase shop, she stared at her and smiled. When she reached her home, Mara came to her house, "Mara?" Josie asked, Mara took the glass vase she bought and smashed her head with it, left the broken glass, and went away...

15th October; Because of Mara's anger and overthinking, with no intention, killed Eric by pushing him into a deep hole...

17th October; After regretting so many deaths, Mara took the officer's gun and shot herself... After knowing about her daughter's death, Mrs. Reia bought poison and killed herself...

Twelve deaths, all happened because of thinking about it and feeling anger, regret, and pain...

What If...?

Does Mara's fate is filled with sadness and bad things? No, she could have a happy life, how?

In the evening, they went for the walk, "Mara, I have something to ask" Eric said in a serious tone, "No lies, tell me the truth, *are you the Killer Queen*" He finally asked, Mara, stopped, she started shaking, "How- HOW DO YOU KNOW!!??" She said angrily. So, it was true, *Mara was the Killer Queen.* Eric was shocked, he stepped back, took his cell phone, and called the police, "NO!! YOU CAN'T!!" She said, "WHY!!??" Eric asked, "I didn't know what to do!? I was blind" Mara started crying, and Eric felt sad, "Mara..." "NO!! NO ONE SHOULD KNOW ABOUT ME!!! Y-YOU CALLED POLICE!?" Mara was again angry, Eric stepped back, "YOU CAN'T DO THAT!!" Mara said, and fell on the ground, "Mara!" Eric came to comfort her, and soon the police came, "Miss. Mara Reia, you are under arrest" Mara looked at officer lake and her hands up, she was scared, and she got handcuffed, "Don't worry Mara..." Eric said...

She was imprisoned for 20 years, "20 years!?" She was shocked and kept in the prison, she regretted her actions and always had a sad face, one day Eric and Mrs. Reia came to meet her, "Mara, don't worry you are not going to be in the prison, we will try our best to bail you out!" They said... Mara tries to smile, and after five years, they could get manage to get the money to bail Mara out, finally, she was bailed out. She was happy than ever, and hugged Mrs. Reia and Eric, "But, my dream is still incomplete, I am never going to be a surgeon" Mara said sadly, "That's why we are going to go to another city!" Mrs. Reia said, a few days later, they shifted, Mara completed her studies and became a surgeon, and tries not to think that she was a murderer and from that day, they lived happily...

An act could have changed a whole ending, who would have thought that? Unfortunately, this ending is not true... In reality, everyone died with a sad ending...

The Characters

MARA REIA
NATALIE REIA
ERIC NELSON
SANDRA MAY
DEREK LAKE

* 9 7 9 8 8 8 9 2 3 7 2 6 6 *